"I think George wants a dinosaur balloon," says Miss Rabbit.
"Alright, how much is it?" Grandpa Pig says.
"Ten pounds please," says Miss Rabbit.

Grandpa Pig thinks the balloon is a bit expensive, but he buys it for George.

"Hold on tight to it," Miss Rabbit says.

Pep[illegible]g™

George's Balloon

Peppa and Georg[redacted]
home with Gra[redacted]
Grandpa Pig when th[redacted]see
Miss Rabbit's ice cream stall.

"Let's stop for ice cream,"
says Granny Pig.
"Why not?" says Grandpa Pig.
"I think we deserve it!"

Peppa, Granny and Grandpa Pig
choose their ice cream.
George is next.
"Dine-saw. Roar!"
says George.

Dine-saw!

But George lets go and
the balloon starts to
float away. Grandpa Pig
quickly grabs the string.

"This is very valuable, George.
I'll hold it on the way home,"
says Grandpa Pig.

Outside Granny and Grandpa's, George plays with his balloon.

"George," says Peppa, "this is an up balloon and if you let it go again it will go up to the moon!"

"Moon!" cries George and he lets the balloon go. The balloon goes up and up but Grandpa Pig catches it just in time.

Peppa and George have gone indoors to keep the balloon safe.

"Hello, Polly," says Peppa. "George has got a new balloon!"

"Squawk!" cries Polly. "Balloon!"
Both Polly and George
love the balloon.

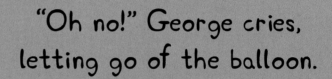

"Oh no!" George cries,
letting go of the balloon.

The balloon floats all
the way out the door, up the
stairs and into the attic.

"Don't worry, it's safe
in here," says Peppa.

“Don’t worry,” says
Granny Pig as they follow
the balloon up the ladder.
“The only way out of the attic
is the window. And the window
is always shut . . .”

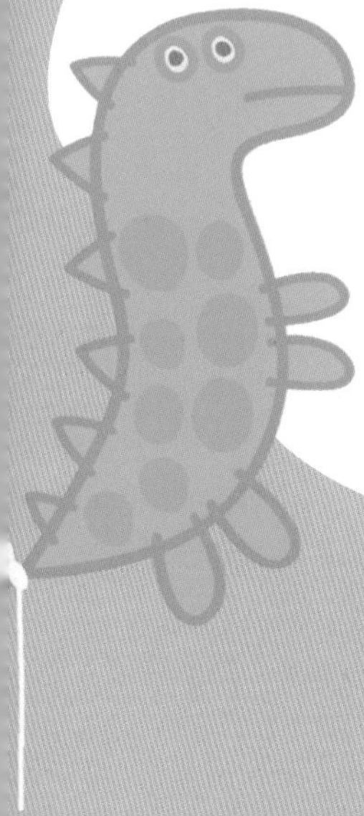

But the window is
not shut. The balloon
escapes outside.

"Your balloon is going to the moon, George," says Peppa.

"Waaah!" cries George. Just then Daddy Pig arrives to take them home. "Oh dear," says Daddy Pig.

Squawk!
Balloon!

"There must be some way
we can get the balloon back,"
cries Granny Pig.

"Squawk! Balloon!"
says Polly Parrot.

Polly flies high up into the sky and catches the balloon string in her beak.

"Polly to the rescue!" cries Grandpa Pig.

Polly Parrot has saved the day.
"Hooray!" George cheers.

"Who's a clever Polly?"
says Granny Pig.

"Who's a clever Polly?"
repeats Polly Parrot.

"George, don't let go of your balloon again," says Peppa.

Daddy Pig has an idea. "I'll tie the balloon to your wrist, George," he says. "That will stop it floating away."

George is very happy.
He loves his balloon. Everyone loves George's balloon. "Snort!"

Snort!
Snort!

Collect these other great Peppa Pig stories

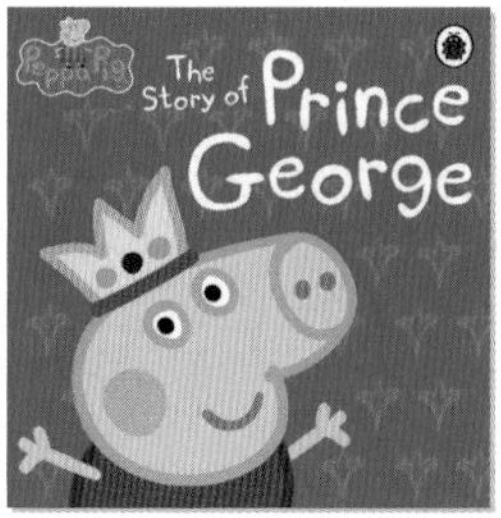